# David Decides
## About Thumbsucking
A Story for Children
A Guide for Parents

by Susan M. Heitler, Ph.D.
Photography by Paula Singer

Published by
Reading Matters
Box 300309
Denver, CO 80203
(303) 757-3506

**Reading Matters,**
**Box 300309, Denver, CO 80203**
**303-757-3506**
**David Decides About Thumbsucking**
**By Susan M. Heitler**
**Photography by Paula Singer**
**Printed by LK Printing Service Inc., Englewood, Colorado**
Library of Congress Catalog Card number 85-61019

**Library of Congress Cataloging in Publication Data**
    Heitler, Susan M. (Susan McCrensky),
1945 -, David decides about thumbsucking.

    "A story for children with a Guide for parents" — Cover.
    Bibliography: p.
    Includes index.
    Summary: Text and photographs follow a young boy as he finds out how to give up the habit of sucking his thumb. Includes a question-and-answer guide for parents and medical professionals.
    1. Finger-sucking — Juvenile literature.
2. Finger-sucking — Psychological aspects-Juvenile literature.

(1. Finger-sucking) I. Singer, Paula,
1943 — , ill. II. Title. (DNLM: 1.
Fingersucking—therapy—popular works.
WS 350.6 H473s)
(HQ784.F5H45 1985)
155.4'22  85-61019
ISBN 0-9614780-2

First U.S. Edition 1985, Reading Matters
Second U.S. Edition 1993, Avon
Third U.S. Edition 1996, Reading Matters

To Abigail, Sara, Jesse and Jacob,
whose struggles with thumb sucking
inspired me to write this book
and whose insights inform these pages.

# David Decides

My name is David.
I want to ask you a hard question.
Have you ever found yourself doing something you like, and not liking that you're doing it?

I have. I like to suck my thumb. It feels good.

When I'm bored, my thumb goes in my mouth. Sucking keeps me busy. When I feel sad, like after a fight with my mom, sucking makes me feel better. When I'm tired, sucking my thumb stops my fussing.

Most of all, at night I suck my thumb to fall asleep.

But... I don't like anyone to see me with my thumb in my mouth.

Sucking is for babies, and I'm getting big.

Still, that thumb does feel good when I want it.
   One night when Dad sat on my bed to kiss me good night he told me, "David, maybe it's time to stop thumbsucking."

I was mad. I put my thumb in my mouth. I pulled the blankets up over my head. In a few minutes, I felt calmer.

Dad leaned toward me.

"David," he whispered, "talk to your sister and brother. Ask them if they ever sucked their thumbs."

The next day I saw my big sister Jennifer at the piano. I sat next to her and listened to her practicing. "Jennifer," I asked, "did you ever suck your thumb?"

Jennifer stopped playing her music. She turned to me and answered, "Lots. See how my top teeth don't match up with my bottom teeth? My thumb pushed the top teeth forward. Now I wear these wires called braces to push the teeth back. I'll have to wear braces this year and probably next year too."

I shivered. I don't want my thumb to push my teeth out of place.

"When did you decide to stop sucking your thumb, Jennifer?" I asked.

Jennifer looked straight into my eyes. "When I was little," she said, "I thought sucking was fine. Whenever I had nothing to do, I used to suck my thumb. Then I started school. That's when I decided to stop. I didn't want anyone to see me sucking like a baby."

I began to worry. When I want to stop sucking will I be able to?

"How did you stop?" I asked Jennifer.

"I really wanted to stop, but my thumb used to go to my mouth without my knowing. So Mom and I decided to cover the thumb with a bandage. The bandage felt funny in my mouth and told me my thumb was there. The bandage made my thumb no good for sucking. After a few weeks, my thumb learned not to go to my mouth. Was I glad!"

I wondered if I would suck my thumb even with a yucky bandage on it. I couldn't imagine not being able to put my thumb in my mouth. What would I do if I was feeling bad? How would I get to sleep at night?

I went to look for my big brother Michael. I found him outside.

"Michael," I asked, "you never used to suck your thumb, did you?"

"Not in the daytime," he answered, "but lots at night."

Even Michael used to have a thumb problem!

12

Michael came over and put his arm around my shoulder. He told me, "I used to suck my thumb to go to sleep. It was still in my mouth when I woke up in the morning. We could tell I had sucked all night because the skin on my thumb looked wrinkled from my wet mouth. The nail on my thumb never needed to be trimmed; I guess nails don't grow so well in mouths. Mom used to say, 'Poor thumbnail–no fresh air to grow tall in.'"

"One night Mom sat on my bed for a long talk about sucking thumbs. We talked about sleep-overs. I didn't want anyone to know I still sucked my thumb, but I did want to go to my friend's house for an overnight. So I decided. Time to stop!"

"How did you keep your thumb out of your mouth?" I asked.

Michael answered, "It was hard. Mom offered to take me to the toy store to pick out something special if I could sleep thirty nights without my thumb. We made a chart to keep count of the nights. On the chart we wrote how many nights I had to sleep without my thumb to earn my prize. Then each night that I made it No Thumbs, we put a star on the chart."

## My Thumbless Nights

|          | Sun. | Mon. | Tues. | Wed. | Thurs. | Fri. | Sat. |
|----------|------|------|-------|------|--------|------|------|
| 1st Week |      |      |       |      |        |      |      |
| 2nd Week |      |      |       |      |        |      |      |
| 3rd Week |      |      |       |      |        |      |      |
| 4th Week |      |      |       |      |        |      |      |

### THE STARS MEAN I'M LEARNING

## What a deal we've made!

If I can sleep _____ nights within the next _____ months without sucking my

thumb I will earn _____!

"Did you have trouble falling asleep without your thumb?" I asked.

Michael answered right away.

"Yes," he nodded his head. "I kept lying there without going to sleep. I felt like something was missing. I really wanted to let my thumb back in my mouth. I locked my hands between my knees. Some nights I hid them under my pillow. Finally sleep would come. But during the night when I was sleeping, my thumb kept going into my mouth again."

"Then what did you do?" I asked him.

"One night at bedtime I cried. I told Dad that stopping sucking was just too hard. I wanted to give up. Dad frowned. He told me, 'If the problem is hard, we have to think harder to solve it.' That's when we came up with out best idea.

"We put socks on my hands."

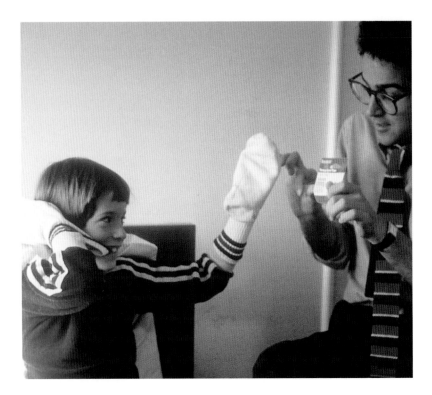

"We taped the socks around my wrists so I wouldn't pull them off while I was sleeping. I reminded Dad every night to help me put on the socks. I kept the tape next to my bed so we wouldn't forget. The socks made my hands sweaty, but they did keep my thumbs out of my mouth. And in the morning if I still had the socks on my hands, I knew I had made it the whole night, No Thumbs.

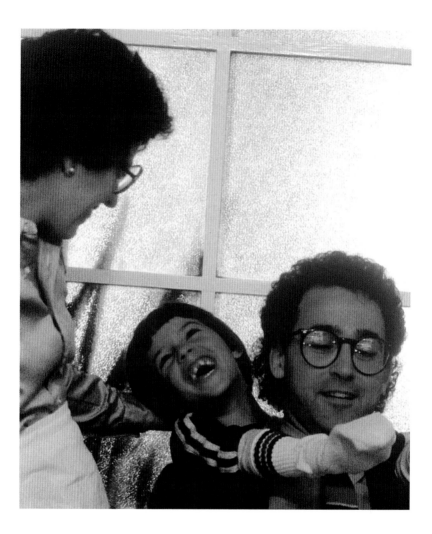

"Then I felt great and ran to show Mom and Dad."

"Did you earn the thirty stars?" I asked.

"Yes! Mom and Dad surprised me with a treat after the first star. After I had earned five stars, they let me stay up late one night to celebrate. After thirty stars, we went to the toy store and I picked out a model airplane," Michael said proudly.

Hearing my sister and brother talk about their thumbsucking made me think. Maybe, just maybe, I might want to stop that habit too.

I went to the mirror in my bathroom. The mirror is tall and I can see all of myself in it.

I am getting big.

I looked at my thumb, and then put it in my mouth. The thumb felt good, but I looked silly. My thumb in my mouth made me look like a baby.

I looked closely at my teeth, thinking if I stop sucking my thumb, stop it real soon, maybe my teeth will stay just the way they are now.

I thought; and looked in the mirror; and thought some more.

My thumb does make me feel good, but do I really need it?

That's it. I've decided. I am going to learn to keep my thumb out of my mouth!

I wonder how long it will take before I don't even want my thumb.

No! I don't care how long it takes. I've decided. Starting today, no more thumbsucking!

Tell me, do you suck your thumb? If you want to stop, maybe this book can give you some ideas. Maybe your mom or dad can help. Mostly though it's up to you.

I know I am ending my thumb habit. Do you want to join me? We can do it!

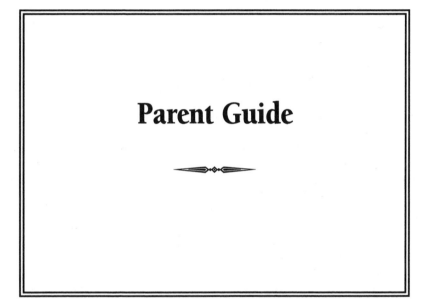

# Parent Guide

# Table of Contents

# Infant Sucking

**How do newborn babies learn to suck?**

Sucking is a newborn's reflexive response to any nipple-shaped object that brushes the baby's cheek or lips. Essential to life, this sucking reflex enables infants to take in nourishment. Without this reflex, babies would starve.

**Why to babies suck on thumbs, fingers, and pacifiers as these do not give forth milk or anything nutritional?**

Sucking comforts an irritable infant, creating a sense of calm and well-being. Pediatricians at Denver's Children's Hospital have monitored infants' breathing, heart rate, digestion, and frequency of crying to understand how these activities are altered by sucking. Irrespective of whether babies prefer a pacifier, finger, or thumb to suck, the action of rhythmic sucking optimizes an infant's breathing and heart rate. Because of this soothing effect, sucking helps a hungry infant wait to be fed, cuts down on fussing when infants are tired, and decreases the time infants spend crying.[1]

The Denver study also showed that muscular movements of the digestive track, called peristalsis, actually work most efficiently when an infant is sucking. When colic or digestive difficulties make a baby uncomfortable, sucking on a breast, bottle, thumb or pacifier re-regulates the intestinal rhythms so the baby's stomach feels more comfortable so that food is digested more smoothly. Other researchers have found similar results. Infants in hospital nurseries cry significantly less if they are given pacifiers between feedings.[2] And infants who suck on thumbs or pacifiers when they seem to feel uncomfortable show fewer symptoms of colic.[3]

As part of the Denver study a group of premature newborns were encouraged to suck on pacifiers or thumbs. The results were quite dramatic. Because sucking optimized infants' breathing and heart rates, reduced the time they spent crying, and enabled them to digest their food more efficiently, the sucking infants put on weight faster, and could leave the hospital sooner then the babies who did not spend time sucking except during feedings.

### Does sucking affect infants' sleep habits?

Thumb and finger sucking babies tend to sleep longer and more soundly than non-sucking infants, apparently because sucking eases the transition from wakefulness to sleep. Infants generally awaken often. Their normal nighttime sleep pattern involves alternation of several sleep hours and then an awake period before sleep is again resumed. Rhythmic sucking lulls them back to sleep.[4]

### Do sucking habits take on new functions as infants grow?

During their first three to six months, healthy babies develop the ability to bring their hands to their mouths. To practice this skill, they bring everything within grasp to their mouths–food, toys, and clothing, as well as fingers and thumbs. Later in the first year, teething may further increase babies' interest in sucking and chewing. Thumbs provide soft "teethers" for tender gums as well as physiological calming.

Interestingly, sucking can be either calming or stimulating. A baby who is agitated can feel soothed with a few minutes of sucking. Because of this calming effect, sucking eases an infant to sleep, and decreases daytime fussiness and crying. Yet a baby who is bored or lonely can perk up with similar sucking.

### Are there differences in emotional development between babies who suck and those who do not?

Psychological research with babies six months to a year old suggests that children who suck their thumbs, fingers, or pacifiers actually may develop more self-confidence than those who do not.[5] Nine-month-olds who have sucking habits crawl further from the mother, and seem to need to spend less time in close body contact with her. Mothers of these infants stay in frequent contact with their children, but are able to do so with words and smiles rather than needing to hold them physically.

### What can I do if my infant seems to want to suck beyond feedings?

When infants seek extra sucking, some mothers offer additional time at the breast. Others encourage use of pacifiers. Some babies discover their fingers or thumbs.

Another option, especially for older infants, is a bottle of water at bedtime. The bottle can be sucked instead of thumbs, fingers, or pacifiers with less likelihood of leading to sucking habits. Bedtime bottles should contain only water. *Sugar-flavored water, juice, or even milk can cause serious decay in baby teeth because the liquid coats the teeth for the night.* Drinking extra fluids in the form of plain water, however, is excellent for babies' health.

**Should I encourage my infant to suck?**

If your infant is fussing, first try to check out the cause. It might be hunger, thirst, a wet diaper, a need to burp, a need for rocking to ease into sleep, or some other discomfort that is the source of distress. Once you have figured out why your baby is crying, rather than immediately offering a thumb or pacifier to stop the sounds of distress, you can respond to the specific need. Your baby may need feeding, burping, rocking, the reassurance of being held, or just a period of crying time to release the day's energy and fall off into sleep.

No parent likes to hear a baby cry. To prevent or hush the sound, as well as to soothe the infant, parents are sometimes tempted to respond too quickly by plugging in a pacifier, thumb, or bottle. This impulse needs to be weighed against the possible long-term difficulties that can develop if a child's sucking is excessively encouraged. Plugging in something to suck may sometimes be the quickest and least energy-consuming response to a fussing infant. In the long run, however, it's worth the effort to expand your repertoire of ways to soothe your baby.

Still, overall, sucking on fingers, thumbs, toes, pacifiers, bottles of water, and toys is healthy and normal in infancy and need not cause parental alarm.

**Which is preferable, a pacifier or thumbsucking?**

Pacifiers and thumbs each have several advantages, and some disadvantages, for infant sucking. The advantages of a pacifier include parents' control over availability, ease of ending the habit, and possibly less damage to the shape of the mouth and therefore to facial appearance. The disadvantages have mainly to do with convenience.

Parents control a pacifier's availability. Therefore, as their infant moves into toddlerhood, parents can gradually limit pacifier use during the day, eventually confining it to the crib for bedtime only. At whatever age they deem appropriate they can eliminate it entirely. Access to thumbs is not as easily controlled.

Although discarding a pacifier is easy, living with the consequences of that action may be temporarily difficult. Even if your child is old enough to discuss the pacifier with you and understand why the time has come to bid it good-bye, a child whose pacifier is no longer available is likely to long for it and to be irritable for several days of adjustment.

After this transition period, however, although some young children do discover that fingers or thumbs can substitute for the missing pacifier, for most, the sucking issue is resolved.

Dental professionals generally agree that intense and frequent sucking of pacifiers, thumbs, or fingers all can affect mouth shape. Research about the relative dental effects in infancy of thumbs versus pacifiers is inconclusive, although the shape of pacifiers is important to note. The baby's mouth is likely to mold to the shape of the pacifier. A long thin pacifier seems to distort mouth shape more than a shorter rounded one that conforms to the natural shape of the inside of the mouth.

While habitual sucking of anything—pacifiers, fingers, or thumbs—can create dental malformations, pacifiers may be less likely to cause pronounced damage because their use is generally discontinued at a younger age. Also, they may exert less pressure against the teeth than thumbs.

On the other hand, babies have to depend on bigger folks to be able to use pacifiers. Because infants in the first months of life cannot grasp and start sucking a pacifier unaided, pacifiers can be a nuisance. Each time the impulse to suck occurs, or the pacifier has fallen out because the baby turned his head or moved about, an adult needs to appear. Many parents find this role burdensome, especially in the middle of the night. By contrast, sucking on fingers or a thumb offers the boon of convenience for both infant and parent. Babies can find and use thumbs whenever they want them, giving the infant more self-sufficiency.

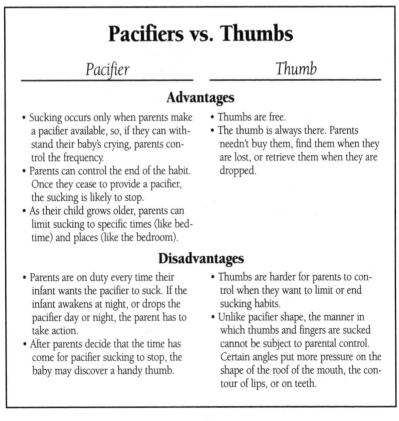

# Pacifiers vs. Thumbs

| *Pacifier* | *Thumb* |
|---|---|
| **Advantages** | |
| • Sucking occurs only when parents make a pacifier available, so, if they can withstand their baby's crying, parents control the frequency. | • Thumbs are free. |
| | • The thumb is always there. Parents needn't buy them, find them when they are lost, or retrieve them when they are dropped. |
| • Parents can control the end of the habit. Once they cease to provide a pacifier, the sucking is likely to stop. | |
| • As their child grows older, parents can limit sucking to specific times (like bedtime) and places (like the bedroom). | |
| **Disadvantages** | |
| • Parents are on duty every time their infant wants the pacifier to suck. If the infant awakens at night, or drops the pacifier day or night, the parent has to take action. | • Thumbs are harder for parents to control when they want to limit or end sucking habits. |
| • After parents decide that the time has come for pacifier sucking to stop, the baby may discover a handy thumb. | • Unlike pacifier shape, the manner in which thumbs and fingers are sucked cannot be subject to parental control. Certain angles put more pressure on the shape of the roof of the mouth, the contour of lips, or on teeth. |

In gaining convenience, parents do lose some control when they elect thumbsucking over pacifiers. By choosing infant nightclothes that can be closed off at the sleeve to seal off tiny fists after the baby has fallen asleep, parents can limit all-night sucking. This limitation, however, makes it harder for babies to put themselves back to sleep without crying for a parent's help when the usual middle-of-the-night awakenings occur. Few parents want to give up the luxury of being able to sleep through the night.

## What do parents need to beware of when their infants use pacifiers?

As previously mentioned, intensive sucking on straight or sausage-shaped pacifiers can cause changes in the arch of the soft bony roof of the mouth, molding it high and narrow around the shape of the pacifier.

In addition, with any pacifier, two common practices can be harmful. Avoid tying the pacifier to a string, or dipping it in something sweet. The convenience of tying a pacifier to a string so your infant can find it more easily is not worth the risk of strangulation, especially after a baby has learned to move around. As to dipping the pacifier in honey or syrup to encourage its use, sugar invites cavities in baby teeth. Because infants and toddlers do not generally receive regular dental checkups, their cavities can progress to the point of causing serious pain and harm.

## Lastly, beware of overuse of pacifiers.

If an infant is not fussing, do not routinely offer a pacifier. You do not want to teach the infant to feel that something is missing if the pacifier isn't there. Also, infants need their mouths free to mimic adults' lip formations of verbal sounds and facial expressions.

## Why does sucking continue after the sucking reflex has been outgrown?

Sucking on something is a mildly pleasant activity and a handy distraction from other less pleasant states. Irritability, discomfort, fatigue, and even mild hunger can be more bearable for a baby who is busily sucking. Any habit that is so pleasant, readily available, and versatile is understandably likely to be continued.

# Toddlers
## Ages One to Three

### Should parents worry about toddler sucking?

Worry, no; notice it, yes. Toddlers commonly suck on fingers and thumbs when they are tired, hungry, bored or upset. This sucking is essentially harmless, generally socially acceptable, and often quite positive. Actually, sucking can help the one-to-three-year-old adjust to his rapidly expanding world, in turn easing his parents' responsibility.

For example, a young child who copes with the challenge of getting to sleep by sucking on a thumb or finger does not need a parent to sit nearby to ease the transition from wakefulness. Sucking is part of the child's movement toward increasing self-sufficiency.

At the same time, sucking too frequently, particularly during the day, is not desirable.

### What aspects of sucking habits do parents of toddlers want to prevent?

Too much of a good thing often spells trouble, and sucking habits fit this rule. Intense sucking throughout the day, or too vigorously all night, can begin to affect the shape of the mouth and facial appearance.

Prevention of excessive sucking by setting thoughtful limits on how often and where sucking occurs can therefore be worthwhile for all children. Though occasional toddler sucking tends to be harmless, preventing too-frequent sucking is often easier than stopping excessive sucking habits once they have become established patterns.

### How can parents limit toddler sucking?

To limit excessive sucking, start by figuring out when, why, and how much sucking takes place. Once the triggers are clear, you can generate alternative

32

solutions. Tailoring your response to the specific problem does take an extra moment of thoughtful attention, but habitually responding to children's fussiness by offering a pacifier encourages children to learn to solve uncomfortable feelings by putting something in their mouths.

Instead, offer a reassuring hug, and seek the reason your child is crying. Did something upsetting happen? Is your child scared? Disappointed? Bored? Tired? Hungry? With your responses aimed at discovering and responding to the underlying difficulty, children learn to deal with distress by problem-solving instead of by mouth-filling.

Many children automatically slip their thumbs into their mouths when they are bored. If you observe in a daycare center or preschool, you will notice how many children put their thumbs into their mouths after they finish one toy or activity, and suck until they become engaged in the next. Parents can decrease wandering-about sucking by helping with the transition into an appealing new activity. Toddlers are generally energetic. They tend, unless tired, to prefer active play to passive sucking. Bring out the crayons and start some coloring. Haul out blocks, or zip up a jacket and head for some fresh air.

Many children suck their thumbs when they are holding a stuffed toy or blanket. They are especially likely to hold a favorite soft object when they feel upset or tired, or are trying to fall asleep. Psychologists refer to these soft animals and blankets as "transitional objects" because they help youngsters to bridge the transition between clinging to parents and feeling more self-sufficient. As one researcher writes, "Many children acquire their strong attachment to a blanket because the hand which is sucked is already grasping some fabric, which literally gets caught up in the sucking habit."[6]

Such sucking "props" can be removed from view and availability during the day. Without the props to trigger the habit, sucking may cease.

A kindly yet firm parental style will help. As you remove the teddy bear or other prop from the living room, you might offer good-humored reminders, such as "Teddy stays in your crib" or "Blankets belong in the bedroom." A toddler soon learns these simply stated and oft-reiterated rules.

The key to implementing props rules is coupling reiteration of rules with clear action. Toddlers, and even preschoolers, generally understand words, but on their own cannot always make the leap from verbal instruction to action. The odds of a cooperative response go up when parents accompany their words with physical movement. If you pick up Teddy and walk him to the crib while you restate the rule "Teddy stays in your crib," your child will soon learn to do the same.

Still, implementing the "props stay in bedrooms" rules may be greeted with resistance. A dose of distraction can help. While you are escorting Teddy back to the crib, for instance, you might engage your child in a discussion of what teddy bears like for breakfast, or begin the transition into another activity by talking about the beautiful sunny sky outside, how the sunshine is beginning to make plants grow...and which jacket would be best for heading outside now.

Story-reading and TV bring out the thumbs for many young children. The glazed-over trance-like state that children enter when they listen to stories or view TV resembles about-to-go-to-sleep restfulness, triggering thumbsucking in children who usually suck as they go to sleep at night.

What can be done when story hour or TV sends children's thumbs into their mouths? At home, parents can help by hugging in a way that holds their child's hand affectionately while they are reading or watching TV together. Children looking at picture books or watching TV alone or in day care can be encouraged to hug a stuffed animal instead of sucking a thumb or fingers.

Parents sometimes try to avert thumb or fingersucking habits by giving toddlers a bottle of milk or juice to carry about the house when their child is getting fussy. As with infants who need something to suck when they go to sleep, a plastic bottle of plain water is a safe and helpful alternative, day or night. Any other liquid can be harmful to new teeth. Parents sometimes find it hard to believe that nutritious milk or juice could be bad for a child; but a steady flow of these liquids invites cavities, swollen gums, yellowing of the teeth, and painful damage to the tooth nerves.

### Are there cautions to heed in trying to limit toddlers' sucking?

Yes. Although limiting toddler sucking can be beneficial, if parents react too strongly they can make sucking worse. Repeated admonishments – "Don't suck your thumb!" – may actually encourage the habit by drawing attention to it. Instead of don'ts, offer dos such as "Let's find something fun for you to do." Most children outgrow sucking spontaneously, especially if their parents neither encourage nor make a big show of discouraging the habit. Parents do best when they couple techniques for minimizing sucking with a general attitude of acceptance.

# Ways to Limit Toddlers' Daytime Sucking

| Likely Causes | Solution Options |
|---|---|
| Boredom | Initiate a new activity. Bring out a toy, books, crayons, or a sweater with which to head outside. |
| Fatigue | Time for a nap. |
| Hunger | Sit down for a snack or meal. Cereal, an apple or grapes, cheese, or milk and a sandwich all beat thumbs for nourishment. |
| Distress | Hugs soothe better than thumbs. After some added verbal reassurance, launching your child back into an engaging activity ends the temptation of the thumb. |
| Presence of objects that remind children of bedtime. | Be sure to couple words and action. As you recite the rule, e.g., "Teddy stays in his crib" or "Blankets belong on beds," accompany your words with removal of the props back to their resting places. Most children then need help shifting their focus elsewhere. "Where are your blocks hiding?" you can ask as you and your child head for the toy box. |

# Preschoolers
## Ages Three to Five

**Do many preschool-age children still suck thumbs or fingers?**

Yes. Studies on the prevalence of thumbsucking suggest that a third to half of three- to five-year-olds suck thumbs or fingers, especially when they are tired.

The amount of time that children spend sucking thumbs or fingers usually decreases spontaneously during this period, and for many preschoolers the habit gradually disappears altogether. One reason may be that by this age most children attend preschool or day care. Away from home, they lack the blankets and teddy bears that accompany their usual sucking habits. Some feel an added incentive; not wanting to appear "babyish" in public, they inhibit the impulse to suck. Nap, story, and bed times, though, still evoke a strong impulse to suck for almost half of youngsters in this age group.

**Why do many preschoolers continue sucking habits instead of sponta-neously outgrowing them?**

Once a child learns sucking as an automatic response to certain situations, the accustomed routine becomes difficult to relinquish. For instance, if a child always sucks his thumb in the drifting time between activities, without suck-ing an uncomfortable feeling will emerge, a feeling that something is missing.

This sensation is similar to what adults feel when someone they love is miss-ing or has died. A search impulse is triggered, an urge to be reunited. Smokers experience a similar impulse when they first try to end a meal without the cus-tomary cigarette. The feeling that something is missing can be intensely uncomfortable. By contrast, with the thumb in place, the child feels normal and complete again.

By this age, children actually derive little gratification from sucking. Habit, plus the discomfort of abstaining, is what keeps them sucking. Children do not necessarily want to suck. Rather, they do not want to experience the distress of not sucking.

## What situations trigger sucking in the preschool years?

In the preschool years any mildly unpleasant feeling can trigger the soothing habit of sucking. Also, situations involving fatigue or restful states will launch sucking impulses.

Around age three children experience an upsurge in their desire for playmates. A child who is alone is likely to feel lonely or incomplete. A thumb in the mouth fills that sense of emptiness and makes longing for social connection more tolerable. But while sucking is easily available, it offers only a minimal solution to the people-hunger of loneliness. Visiting a friend, playing with siblings, or going to mother for a hug are more gratifying for the child and help develop better social habits for later life.

Sucking combats boredom by inducing a meditative physiological state. When children sit quietly sucking a thumb, they may look passive, but they are doing something; they are producing physical sensations. Again, the sucking solution is easily accessible, but only minimally gratifying. Lively preschoolers need activity and stimulation. Toys, games, friends, or outdoor exploration are preferable.

Unpleasant feelings like sadness, pain, and anxiety may lead preschoolers to slip their thumbs into their mouths. Rhythmic sucking is an alternative to crying, and may be soothing; but affectionate concern expressed by a friend or a caring adult is more comforting.

Children of preschool age need to learn to communicate their thoughts and emotions, but sucking gets in the way of talking. Instead of plugging up their mouths when they are upset, children need to learn to verbalize feelings. If they can say, "I feel sad," "I'm disappointed," or "I'm mad," the odds go up that they will succeed in finding solace from friends, teachers, or family members. Similarly, preschoolers who continue to use thumbsucking to delay response to basic biological needs such as hunger, fatigue, or the need to urinate need to learn to verbalize that they want something to eat, need to rest, or have to go to the bathroom.

Like the famous image of Linus and his blanket, for many youngsters the sight and feel of a favorite blanket or stuffed animal triggers sucking. Interestingly, the opposite is also true. When children end their sucking habits, they usually lose interest in their blanket and animal sucking props. In one study of eight children, seven ceased their attachment to the soft objects when they stopped sucking their thumbs.[7]

As with toddlers, television viewing triggers sucking in many preschoolers.

The semiconscious trance induced by a television, so similar to bedtime's drift toward unconsciousness, provokes bedtime-like behaviors. Preschoolers, like toddlers, need clear rules keeping blankets and stuffed animals separate from television viewing. They also may benefit from a house rule stating that thumbsucking isn't allowed with TV watching. In some households, parents establish the rule "When the thumb is in, the TV goes off." Children soon learn to sit on the thumb or lock it between their knees to keep it from heading, self-propelled, into sucking position.

Finally and most commonly, preschoolers suck their thumbs because sucking helps them fall asleep. Once asleep, some children leave their thumbs in their mouths all night, sucking periodically and often quite vigorously until morning. Other children resume sucking in the early morning hours to prevent full awakening. Sleep-related sucking thus may occur at bedtime, throughout the night, or in the evening and then early morning. Children who suck to fall asleep may also suck during the day if they feel tired.

### Is sucking "contagious"?

Yes. Some children who never sucked as infants discover the habit in later years when they are exposed to the example of sucking playmates. Preschool and day-care programs, while helpful for children and essential for working parents, do bring many children together. Less desirable habits may be communicated.

Fortunately, when children develop sucking habits after age three the habits seem to be relatively easy to snuff out, particularly if parents and teachers initially respond with a clear and firm message that sucking is out of bounds. Intense finger or thumbsucking habits begun in early infancy may be difficult to bring to a halt, but with late-onset sucking, simply explaining to a child that sucking is a potentially harmful habit frequently suffices.

The harder case is when children who have been sucking only at bedtime expand their sucking after frequent exposure to children who suck throughout the day. If these children do not respond when parents explain that expanding their sucking can hurt their appearance, then it may be best to ignore expansion of sucking into daytime hours until the child is closer to kindergarten age. After age five, for a number of reasons, children more easily end the habit.

### Do preschoolers cause their teeth to move, decreasing their facial attractiveness, by sucking thumbs or fingers?

Often, yes, particularly if the sucking is vigorous. One dental researcher estimates that for approximately 20 percent of thumbsucking four- and five-year-olds, the effect on teeth is problematic by causing the upper teeth to protrude and harming the bite, that is, the way the upper and lower teeth make contact.[8]

Occasional gentle sucking is unlikely to mold teeth or mouth shape. Children who do not create strong suction, but rather just dangle fingers or a thumb in their mouths. probably suffer less dental damage. Many children do habitually suck in this casual manner. By contrast, vigorous frequent sucking on thumbs or fingers can profoundly alter facial appearance.

When children put a finger or thumb in their mouths, the digit may press against the roof of the mouth. This pressure can be intensified by strong sucking. Together, the suction and the pressure can create an opening between the top and bottom teeth molded to the shape of the fingers or thumbs. Dentists call this opening "overjet" and/or "open bite" depending on the particular way the teeth are moved.

Because vigorous sucking puts pressure on the roof of the mouth, it also can change the shape of the soft-bone structure inside the mouth. The roof of the mouth may be pushed upward and the sides of the roof narrowed. Dentists call this condition "crossbite" because it causes the upper side teeth to cross over and sit inside, rather than directly above, the lower back teeth.

Movement of baby teeth from thumbsucking can cause problems with permanent teeth because baby teeth forge the paths the permanent teeth take into their positions. If upper front baby teeth have been pushed forward (proclined) and lower front baby teeth pushed back (retroclined), adult teeth are likely to grow similarly. Continuation of sucking after the arrival of permanent teeth makes these conditions worse.

## Can the changes in appearance from thumbsucking be for the better?

Young children with a flared upper lip and protruding upper teeth can look cute. Though "cute" in children, however, these changes do not correlate with what most adults find attractive in other adults. And a twisted front tooth, or a wide space between front teeth created by thumb or finger pressures during sucking, detracts from appearance at all ages. Especially if a child will not have the benefit of corrective orthodonture, prevention is highly worthwhile.

## Can sucking cause speech defects?

Although the data is not completely clear on this question, there are indications that sucking can accentuate potential speech problems. In particular, preschoolers who suck fingers or thumbs may lisp in a manner created by a condition called "tongue thrust."

Tongue thrust refers to a mode of sealing the mouth for swallowing by thrusting the top of the tongue forward against the lips. Tongue thrust is a normal swallowing reflex among infants, but usually disappears with the arrival of teeth. Children who continue infant sucking habits past their toddler years sometimes also continue to use this more primitive swallowing mode. Tongue thrust exerts pressure on the front teeth, increasing the likelihood that the teeth will be pushed out and also interfering with the correct formation of certain speech sounds

## Can sucking on fingers hurt the growth of the finger as well as the appearance of teeth and lips?

Yes. Thumbs seem to develop normally even if they are vigorously sucked, but sucking on fingers, particularly if continued past the age of five, can deform the growing finger.[9,10,11]

A frequently and strongly sucked finger may grow in a rotated direction, or may appear twisted ("hyperextension"). In these cases, once sucking is ended, the finger deformity may spontaneously correct. In at least two of five extreme cases described in one research report, however, the children required surgery in order to return the finger to a normal shape. Without the surgery, holding a pencil was not possible because of the rotation of the finger.

Interestingly, girls seem to be at higher risk than boys for damage to the growth of a finger from prolonged fingersucking.[12] Researchers hypothesize that boys receive more social pressure to end sucking habits once they start elementary school, sparing them from the more permanent harm that can be caused to sucked fingers.

## Can daytime sucking affect social development?

Sucking blocks the communication channel. A child with a thumb or finger in his mouth cannot talk. A sucking child may learn a pattern of avoiding confrontation by turning away and sucking a thumb. Children instead need to develop assertiveness skills. They need to learn to tell Johnny, "It's my turn on the tricycle," rather than sucking a thumb for self-consolation, and giving up on trying to get what they want.

Sucking can, in a subtle way, interfere with the development of friendships. Sucking initiates retreat into an inner world of thoughts and feelings that excludes peers, parents, and teachers. Shy children in particular often find this retreat easier than attempting to socialize, even if they yearn for friendships.

While shyness may cause a retreat into sucking, sucking in turn can perpetuate a child's feeling like an outsider. An astute observer of a preschool classroom or playground can sometimes see a quiet ostracism of thumbsucking children. In a generally friendly group, other children are unlikely to tease children who suck, but they are likely to ignore them. Perhaps they see the behavior as babyish and unattractive; or they may be responding to the thumbsuckers' message that they are unavailable for social interaction. If emotional upsets are triggering the sucking, other children may sense that this child is troubled and will not be fun to play with. Whatever the underlying reasons, children who suck their thumbs at school are more likely to be left on the outskirts of the social network. Once a child stops sucking the stigma seems to disappear.

One research study[13] has found particularly striking data in this regard. Researchers monitored the social activity of preschool children who sucked their thumbs, counting the number of times they talked or played with other children. They then helped the thumbsuckers to end their habit. When thumbsucking had ceased, they again counted each child's number of social interactions. After sucking had been ended, children became more outgoing, initiating and receiving more interactions with both friends and teachers.

## Can thumb and fingersucking increase risks to physical health?

Sucking raises health concerns as a child's world begins to expand beyond the familiar environment of home. Thumb and fingersucking increases exposure to colds, and illnesses. When a thumb or finger enters the mouth, so does everything on it, plus dirt under nails. In preschool or day-care homes where many children touch the same toys, germs pass from hand to toy to hand. Repeated strep and staph infections can occur from thumbsucking, because germs under the nails of thumbs and fingers are not touched by systemic antibiotics.[14]

Several intestinal parasites enter the body through the mouth. Pinworm, for instance, spreads readily in American daycare centers and nursery schools. Though easily treated and not an ailment of major serious concern, pinworm does create unpleasant symptoms such as itching around the anal area, stomachache, waking at night (when the worms are more active), decreased appetite, and irritability (perhaps from loss of sleep and appetite).

Although children who do not suck their thumbs also can ingest germs and parasites, thumbsucking does increase the risk.

Risk of lead poisoning may also increase when children put thumbs or fingers in their mouths.[15] Lead poisoning poses a particular danger to city children who live in traffic-congested areas. Small particles of lead emitted by car-exhaust fumes settle in the dust on floors and furniture and outdoors on sidewalks and playgrounds. Even in minute quantities lead is toxic, particularly to young children. Mounting evidence indicates that inner-city children who absorb undue amounts of lead show subtle evidence of brain damage demonstrated by hyperactivity, perceptual handicaps, and reduced intellectual functioning.

## Is sucking a sign of emotional disturbance in preschoolers?

No. Most sucking in the preschool years is a simple, comfortable habit, and not a sign of emotional disturbance. Multiple studies have clearly established that thumbsucking children are no more likely to be disturbed or emotionally needy than non-suckers.[16,17]

Still, thumbsucking children are certainly not exempt from emotional difficulties. In instances where disturbing situations at home, day care, or school are causing upset, unusual sucking patterns can signal a child's distress. A child who sucks his thumb in isolation for long periods each day or who fre-

41

quently runs to find a blanket and slip his thumb into his mouth may be unhappy.

When there is pervasive daytime sucking, or an unexplained sudden increase in the frequency of sucking, parents and teachers may find it helpful to consult with a psychological professional to assess what is causing the upset and to determine how the problem can be eased.

## What if children twist and pull out their hair as part of their sucking habit?

Hair loss, known by doctors as alopecia, can occur if children pull on their hair to accompany their thumb or fingersucking. Ending the sucking habit usually ends the hair loss problem. If not, consult a doctor; medication such as clomipramine hydrochloride may be helpful for eliminating continued hair-pulling.[18]

# Kindergarten
## Age Five

Children approaching the age of five who are still sucking on thumb or fingers are likely to need someone—parents, a relative, a teacher, or a dentist—to offer information and incentives to start bringing the habit to an end.

**Why is age five the magic age for encouraging children to end sucking habits?**

As children grow older, sucking habits become an increasing social and dental liability. By the time a child is turning five, sucking creates more problems than it solves.

Past age five, daytime sucking is a social no-no. Children who continue to suck in public look childish to their peers.

The eruption of permanent teeth that starts at about age six heralds serious consequences for facial appearance if the sucking continues.[19] Few factors are as important to self-esteem as attractive appearance. And few factors have such dramatic impact on others' initial responses to someone as how attractive that person looks.

The good news is that cognitive changes occur about age five. The changes that make children ready to leave preschool and able to handle the demands of elementary school also enable a child to muster the self-control to conquer sucking habits. By this age children usually understand cause and effect. They can comprehend that although sucking may be pleasant, it may also be harmful. They have the maturity to understand that the consequences of sucking, although gradual, are real.

# School-Age Children
## Ages Six to Twelve

**Do many school-age children still suck thumbs and fingers?**
The percentage of children who suck on thumbs or fingers drops off sharply as children enter and proceed through elementary school. Research suggests that approximately 13 percent of six-year-olds continue the habit, but in the seven-to eleven-year-old group only about 6 percent of children are still sucking, and these do so mainly to fall asleep at night.[20]

**How do school-age children feel about sucking habits?**
By first grade, few children want to be seen thumb or fingersucking.
What children do in the privacy of their home is another matter. When they return from school, children may slip into comfortable sucking as soon as they pass through the front door. Even more sustain the habit when they lie down at bedtime. They still depend on sucking a thumb to ease the transition from wakefulness to sleep. And they may unknowingly continue to suck throughout the night.

**What are the dental consequences of sucking for an older child?**
Past age six and with the arrival of permanent teeth, serious dental consequences from habitual sucking are almost inevitable, particularly if a child's teeth are not perfectly aligned to begin with. One Norwegian study of 167 thumbsuckers found that 87 percent had a malocclusion needing correction.[22] In another large study, this one of 689 Canadian children, 52 percent of those whose teeth were poorly aligned were assessed to have problems that were directly attributable to sucking habits.[23]
Moreover, past age four or five, and particularly once permanent teeth have erupted, children are unlikely to find that the changes in their altered teeth

44

and bite positions will improve spontaneously.

Fortunately, orthodonture can remedy many unattractive tooth positions. Still, though clearly helpful for many children (and adults), orthodonture entails significant costs in discomfort, temporarily decreased attractiveness, and major financial outlay. When financial or other considerations preclude the option of orthodonture, changes in appearance from sucking habits may affect appearance for a lifetime.

Orthodonture often creates dramatic improvements in the appearance of children who have been thumbsuckers. Nonetheless, if children continue to suck thumbs or fingers beyond age six, they risk development of dental malformations that orthodontic treatment cannot reverse. In these extreme cases surgical techniques can sometimes re-form the mouth structure to pre-sucking appearance, but prevention is clearly preferable.

### Is thumbsucking a sign of abnormal psychological development in school-age children?

Whereas it may be helpful in infancy, and common if not particularly beneficial in the preschool years, daytime thumbsucking becomes a warning sign suggesting possible developmental difficulties in school-age children. Multiple studies suggest that the older the thumbsucking child, the more likely that family problems, excessively scolding or punitive parenting, excessively permissive parenting, or other sources of either emotional distress or parenting difficulties are hindering a child's development.[24]

### What are the social consequences of thumbsucking for school-age youngsters?

If children six or older suck at school or with friends, they look odd. Peers view them with surprise, and are likely to comment. In one study researchers found that other grade-school children do not want thumbsucking children as friends, seatmates, or even classmates .[21]

The social consequences affect boys more strongly than girls. Boys who suck during the day look "sissyish" to their peers. They risk becoming social outcasts and victims of teasing if they continue the habit in public. Girls may risk less overt social humiliation with the habit, but can expect to be regarded as out of the norm.

Those boys and girls who still enjoy a thumb or fingersucking habit in private are likely to try to keep the now-embarrassing pastime a secret. The costs of sucking by this point clearly outweigh the minor emotional comfort of sucking, but the habit may still feel difficult to break. Supportive help from parents can make a big difference by enabling these children to feel that curbing the habit is a feasible, genuine option.

**Given the consequences, why do parents allow older children to continue sucking habits?**

Many parents erroneously believe that there is little they can do to influence a child to stop. They think the habit must be outgrown spontaneously.

Other parents believe, also erroneously, that sucking meets a deep psychological need. This Freudian-based idea used to be common among both psychologists and dentists, but it is less prevalent now and has been discredited by research.

When parents who sense that their child should be outgrowing thumbsucking are also concerned that breaking the habit may have dire emotional consequences, their ambivalence can confuse a child, undermining any efforts to curb the sucking. Ambivalence is particularly likely if parents interpret sucking as a sign that their child needs sucking to compensate for their inadequacies as parents. Parents may be understandably reluctant to put an end to sucking if they believe the habit signifies that they have been unsuccessful at satisfying their child's needs. Still, such reluctance is seldom appropriate. Studies have concluded that, in older children, sucking is more likely to create emotional problems than to offer solace.

A variety of other reasons may prevent a parent from intervening effectively. Some parents have an ideological commitment to permissive child-rearing. Some parents don't want to give up having a "baby" at home. Some may feel helpless and experience the child as not within their control. Others try a harshly authoritarian approach that stiffens the child's resistance. Still others carry such a heavy load of obligations that they simply overlook the sucking or put off dealing with it. If parents work long hours, juggle extensive community responsibilities, take care of the needs of many young children, or struggle with health, financial, or relationship difficulties, sucking may take a backseat to more immediate crises.

Whatever parents' reasons for not intervening, I advise considering the potentially serious consequences of thumbsucking in older children. Sucking beyond preschool is a vestigial habit that provides only minimal emotional sustenance, and at considerable cost.

**Do older children who are having a hard time emotionally, and who also happen to be thumbsuckers, need the sucking habit?**

Especially for these children, habitual sucking after age five may create more harm than help. Sucking can provide mild soothing to calm a distressed child. And stopping the habit requires quite a bit of emotional energy. Still, these children have enough difficulties already, and certainly do not want to add decreased facial attractiveness. In addition, disturbed children, like emotionally healthier kids, need friendship. Children with problems often can least afford the social stigma of daytime thumbsucking.

Orthodontists have observed that emotionally distressed children tend to develop more severe orthodontic problems than their more emotionally comfortable peers.[25] They suspect that when children feel distressed they suck more vigorously, for longer periods, and more frequently—just the factors that increase risk of dental harm from sucking.[26]

Still, considerations of timing, of when to initiate a thumb-stopping program, may be important for children who are emotionally stressed. Certainly, when a child is engulfed by an acute crisis, taking on challenges one at a time makes sense. Tackling thumbsucking may need to be put on a back burner if clearly stressful events are occurring, such as a child's parents deciding to separate, a sibling falling ill, or an upsurge of financial problems.

## What are the emotional and social consequences of ending sucking habits?

According to mothers' ratings in a study with sixty-six thumbsucking children, those who ended their thumbsucking habits found it easier to make and keep friends than those who continued the habit.[27] Mothers reported that ending the sucking in itself seemed to lead to more interactions with friends and with teachers.

Another study explored whether ending sucking habits might lead to substitution of other, more serious tension-reduction habits. Twenty-two children ages four to twelve were assisted in ending sucking habits. A control group of forty-three other children of the same ages were also followed. Of the twenty-two children who stopped the sucking, five did develop tendencies to chew on clothing or bite their nails, but these are mild habits, not harmful to dentition and less socially unacceptable than thumbsucking for older children.

An additional finding quite surprised these researchers. They found that in the control group of forty-three children who were allowed to continue their sucking habits, more serious behaviors such as increased handling of genitals developed. It appeared that stopping the thumbsucking actually seemed to decrease the development of more serious nervous habits.[28]

The conclusion, then, of many dental and psychological researchers is that a child older than five or six who continues sucking his thumb, especially in public situations, needs to end the behavior. Past a certain age sucking is no longer either cute, normal, or socially acceptable.[11,29]

# Adolescents and Adults

When the *Wall Street Journal* in the late 1980s ran a front-page feature on adult thumbsucking, the article evoked considerable surprise. Orthodontists, however, have long seen a significant number of thumbsucking adolescents and adults. Their habits usually have been discontinued in public, but in private the childhood habit has persisted.

The impact of these additional years of sucking on teeth and facial structure can be worrisome; the impact on self-esteem also can be significant. Adolescents' and adults' sucking, though pleasant and comforting, is usually kept hidden as an embarrassing secret, and keeping secrets has its costs.

# Helping Children to End Sucking Habits

**I want my child to stop sucking. What can I do?**

*David Decides* can help parents to introduce the idea that sucking habits need to end in an uncritical, upbeat way. The story was written to motivate children to want to end sucking habits, and to demonstrate techniques for stopping. This way, rather than feeling like a parent is making them stop, children feel like the choice is their own. They then can end the habit with a sense of accomplishment and pride.

**Has the story been tested?**

In an informal study in an Alabama dental practice, Dr. Charles Hall gave *David Decides* to fifty children five years of age and older. Ninety-six percent successfully ended the habit within three weeks.

Dr. Hall thinks the story works because it shows children how to stop the habit themselves, yet at the same time shows parents how to be effective in supporting the child.

**How does the *David Decides* story work?**

The intent of the story is multifold: to give children information that encourages the choice to end sucking; to offer practical suggestions that help with the frustrations of trying to end the habit; and to bolster confidence that the habit can be conquered.

David's parents begin by making David aware of the problems sucking can cause. That information gives David the motivation he needs to decide to end the habit.

David's parents select a quiet time, before bedtime, to initiate a thumbsucking discussion. Bedtime can be a particularly good setting to read David's story to your child. Children seem to use David's example best if the story is read to them several times.

*David Decides* encourages children to take responsibility for deciding whether, when, and how they will stop. Parents can increase the impact of the story by asking their child questions. What made David choose to end his habit? What does your child think of David's decision? Well-chosen after-story questions help children to digest the story and make their own sucking decision.

If children feel that the decision to stop sucking has been made by their parents, subsequent parental attempts to help with ending the habit, though intended to be supportive, may feel coercive. Neither parents nor children usually want a parent-child battle of wills. Reluctance and resentment may result if parents' help decreases their children's sense of having chosen themselves to end thumbsucking. By contrast, when children feel that the decision to stop thumbsucking has been their own, parents are more likely to find their children seeking their assistance.

Once a child clearly wants to stop sucking, parent and child can work together with enthusiasm to end the habit. Still, if parents' help is provoking resentment or resistance, parents may need to recede into the background. All along the way, children do best if they sustain the understanding that ending sucking habits is their project, not their parents'.

### Do children need help once they have decided to stop sucking?

Many do. Some children can overcome sucking by sheer will-power. Others, motivated by their new understanding of the habit's potential consequences to their appearance, lose all interest in sucking. Most children though, like most adults, find changing an entrenched habit very challenging.

Adults struggling with overeating, alcoholism, or smoking habits frequently can be helped by what psychologists call behavior modification techniques. Children also can benefit from a simple behavior-modification plan. Once your child has made a decision to halt sucking, a set of rewards can keep the goal in focus. Rewards for success bolster determination, boost enthusiasm, and increase the odds of success.

### How do behavior modification techniques work?

Most skills children master as they grow up offer intrinsic rewards. Learning to walk or to talk enlarges a child's world, offering increased enjoyment. Learning to read brings the pleasure of an unfolding story. No such joys come from learning to end sucking habits. The child who is trying to reach this goal experiences only frustration. Behavior modification helps to sustain a child's persistence by offering external rewards to compensate for the lack of intrinsic rewards.

What rewards work in a behavior-modification program? Parental appreciation may be enough. Praise and hugs certainly reinforce a child's determination. Concrete rewards, though, tend to be more powerful incentives for youngsters. The promise of a longed-for toy, a special privilege, or a desirable outing can be highly motivating. In *David Decides*, David's brother Michael earns a model airplane. Another child might prefer a later bedtime, an overnight trip, or a special day with a parent. In general, the most successful goal choices are those suggested by the child. The more pervasive the sucking habit, the more tempting and powerful the reward will need to be.

Sometimes the formality of the term "behavior modification" misleads parents. In fact, this strategy may work most effectively when approached as a fun challenge. Used in a playful way, a system of rewards for successfully overcoming the temptation to keep sucking just stacks the odds on the side of success.

### Is "behavior modification" really just a fancy term for bribery?

Yes and no. Both bribes and incentives encourage people to do things they otherwise might not undertake. A bribe, however, convinces someone to do something that is not right. The rewards in a behavior modification program, by contrast, strengthen resolve and accomplish goals that are positive.

### Why does David's mother set up a chart to record his progress?

Keeping a record of successes motivates children to stick with their anti-sucking campaign. Successful thumb-less days and nights can be starred, circled, or indicated with stickers on a chart or calendar. This evidence of progress becomes a reward in itself.

The chart also gives both parent and child a way of determining when goals have been attained and awards earned. Any calendar can be used, or parents can draw up a chart with their child. Specifying dates helps to prevent confusions about which days have been recorded.

In *David Decides*, David and his mother write down the terms of his no-sucking agreement, specifying the length of time and the reward. Writing the specifics of the plan serves several purposes. Committing the agreement to writing tends to move the child from a vague desire to be sucking-free to a clear decision. Public commitment increases the likelihood of success. And writing down the specifics of the agreement prevents later misunderstandings about what reward was promised for what accomplishment.

### How often should rewards be given?

Younger children usually need more frequent payoffs, especially at the outset of the project. A five-year-old is likely to be enthused by a small but special reward after the difficult first night. A little gift or a special treat that morning to celebrate the first steps of progress can make the far-ahead goal seem less distant. Reward periods can gradually be stretched out to several nights, every week, and eventually to attainment of thirty nights without sucking.

## What can children do when they catch themselves sucking?

When children discover their hands near their faces, or even with the thumb or finger back in its familiar mouth position, they can say, "Good for me—I caught it!" This response energizes them to respond effectively.

Once children have become aware of the sucking and have praised themselves for the discovery, a "habit reversal" technique may help. If they can pull the offending thumb or finger away from the mouth, and then make a fist, grasping the finger or thumb in the fist becomes a competing action that inhibits continued sucking. A study comparing this technique with painting the thumb with a bitter-tasting substance showed that the habit-reversal technique significantly boosted children's success rates.[30]

The key to effective use of making a fist to hold the problematic thumb or finger is practice. Children can pretend to find their thumb or finger back in its mouth position, and then pull it out, praise themselves, and make a fist. This practice makes success with the technique all the more likely.

## How long does it take to end sucking habits?

A first attempt to break the habit is likely to take two weeks to two months of focused, playful attention.

After reading *David Decides,* some children end the habit on the spot. For others the project goes very slowly. They may not lose the impulse to suck until they have collected as many as several thirty-night awards. The habit can be remarkably persistent.

Parents usually err on the side of underestimating the length of time required to break this habit. An underestimation sets up parents and children to feel discouraged if their mistaken expectations lead them to feel they have failed. Realistically, the impulse to suck may still arise after thirty or even sixty successful days.

Even then, the sucking impulse may reemerge from time to time. Additional briefer periods of focusing on the habit may be needed before the impulse to suck is eliminated altogether.

## What do parents find most difficult while their children are trying to end sucking habits?

For many parents, the hardest aspect of implementing a behavior modification program is sustaining the record-keeping. If the chart is highly visible, and placed so that it catches the parent's eye during the daily routine, it is more likely to be maintained. Some parents tape it to the refrigerator door. Others attach it near the bed to be marked when the child goes to sleep (for daytime sucking) or awakens (for night sucking).

Helping a child overcome sucking habits requires patience, good humor, and time. A parent who is feeling harried and overloaded from other concerns may be best off waiting until a calmer period.

## What other pitfalls can discourage parents who implement a behavior-modification program?

One common mistake is launching a reward program before a child has been sufficiently motivated. If a child has not yet firmly decided that he wants to give up sucking, any attempts are doomed. Motivation is crucial.

A second common tendency is for parents to become too involved when thumbs or fingers do inadvertently enter the child's mouth. Frequent repetition, no matter how kindly, of "Take your thumb out, please" can be counterproductive. The child, not the parent, must learn to control the habit. On the other hand, occasional good-humored comments that bring sucking activity to the child's attention can be helpful. Caution is the rule. Children who feel nagged begin to regard the parent as an antagonist rather than as an ally in the fight against sucking.

Because sucking habits can be so exasperatingly persistent, parents may be tempted to succumb to irritated frustration. Beware. Ridicule and angry criticism can break down cooperation and make a child resentful. They do sometimes motivate children to succeed just to prove the parent wrong, but an angry strategy poses significant risks. Children can respond by developing a negative self-image and bad feelings toward the parent who hurt their feelings. And when parents lose patience, their discouragement can be contagious. By contrast, drawing attention to successes, instead of dwelling on failures, increases a child's hopefulness and determination.

## What if sucking is triggered by multiple cues?

When sucking is very frequent, it can be harder to conquer. If a child sucks day and night, when hungry, tired, bored, upset, or idle, tackling the problem in manageable chunks may be advisable. The first target perhaps could be sucking outside the home, or sucking in front of the television. Other daytime sucking could be eliminated next, with bedtime sucking reserved as the final challenge.

## What initial frustrations do children face as they try to break a sucking habit?

A child's first days without sucking are generally the most difficult. The longing to put that thumb where it feels comfortable and comforting can become intense. Like grief from other losses, however, this longing gradually diminishes and eventually fades away.

Parents can help sustain the child's determination through this challenging initial period with reassurance, appreciation, and rewards. They may also need to summon up extremes of patience and tolerance to cope with the child's temporarily increased irritability.

**How can children become aware when thumbsucking is occurring?**

Thumbs and fingers have a remarkable ability to travel to the mouth on automatic pilot. Habitual thumbsuckers seldom realize when their thumb is in action. Gentle reminders from parents may be helpful if they do not make the child defensive. Preferably, though, children need to find a way to become aware when sucking is beginning without needing to depend on parents.

A variety of simple options are likely to be welcomed provided they are presented as options available for children to choose to utilize if they want–not as something done to a child.

One easy solution is to cover the sucking thumb or fingers with a bandage. Because the bandage feels awkward and tastes odd, it brings immediate awareness. Bandages have another advantage. Because they are common and carry no social stigma, they can be worn to school to protect against daytime sucking.

Some parents coat thumbs with hot sauce or a bitter-tasting solution marketed

---

# Do's and Don'ts to Help Your Child End Thumb and Fingersucking

| Do | Don't |
|---|---|
| Pick a time when life is proceeding with relative calm to launch the habit-breaking process. Begin by reading the "David Decides" story together. | Pick a time when you or your child are already feeling overloaded with other concerns. This habit can be a stickler and may need considerable attention to overcome. |
| Discuss the potential consequences of the habit. Ask your child to explain to you the problems sucking can cause. Once children understand how sucking can affect their appearance, they usually choose to end the habit. | Assume that your child understands the impact of sucking on facial appearance. |
| Encourage your child to identify when sucking occurs, i.e., what situations and feelings trigger the automatic thumb-to-mouth movement. | Assume your child knows when the sucking occurs. Thumbs travel to mouths by automatic pilot. Children are often surprised to discover when they are sucking, and that there are specific patterns. |

| **Do** | **Don't** |
|---|---|
| Appreciate that the thumbsucking is well-intended. Sucking can soothe distressed feelings, offer stimulation in response to boredom, and ease the transition from wakefulness to sleep. It's just a costly way to accomplish these goals. | Criticize or belittle the thumbsucking. |
| Brainstorm with your child to determine alternatives for each specific habitual sucking situation.<br>• If boredom triggers sucking, children can learn to say to an adult, "What can I do now?"<br>• If the cue is watching TV, children can hold a glass of water or sit on their hands.<br>• If sucking occurs at bedtime, children can tuck their hands under the pillow or between their knees.<br>• For through-the-night sucking, children can tape a sock over the hand with the sucking thumb. | Succumb to the mistaken belief that the child needs the sucking. Other, less harmful responses can accomplish the same objectives. |
| If the sucking still occurs, sympathize with how hard it is to end a persistent habit. | Criticize, nag or label your child in negative ways, though occasional firm insistence that the habit must stop can bolster a child's flagging determination. |
| After the sympathy, join together in more thinking. What additional measures might help? | Assume the situation is hopeless. |
| If you add a behavior modification chart with stars indicating successes and a prize at the end, be sure to keep the chart in a handy place where record-keeping will be easy. | Forget to record successes. If you are having trouble remembering to put up stars, maybe another family member can assist, or the thumbsucking child can be responsible for reminding the parent to record daily stars. |
| Remember, the enemy is the habit not the child. | Get into a power struggle. Parent and child need to be allies, not enemies. Parent and child need to unite against the problem, not fight each other. |

commercially for this purpose. Such liquids can be painful if they are rubbed into the eye, so parents of young children should be cautious with this option.

Playful approaches work well for some children. A parent may paint a face on the thumb or cover it with a knitted puppet secured at the base with tape.

A tongue depressor or stick of any kind can be taped to the thumb like a little cast. Because this technique is foolproof, a child who is determined to stop sucking may find several days of it reassuring. On the other hand, the restriction of movement can be irritating.

To help prevent nighttime sucking, a lightweight mitten, glove, or sock can be taped around the wrist so it will not be pulled off unconsciously. Although it may get sweaty, a covered hand frees the child from concern about sucking during the night, and in the morning offers proof of a thumb-free night.

### What if a child gets too discouraged to continue?

Even with the best of intentions plus supportive parents, children some-times become too frustrated to continue an anti-sucking program. They may be too young to stop, overwhelmed by too many stresses running concurrently in their lives, or just not yet ready for whatever reason.

In these cases, drop the focus on the sucking for a period of time. An extended vacation from the anti-sucking program will help everyone relax. After several months, a freshly enthusiastic run on the challenge may feel much easier. Leaving the project for a while renews everyone's energy for a second try at reading the *David Decides* story and making the No More Thumbsucking decision.

### What can parents do if they see a successfully conquered habit begin to reemerge?

Children who have stopped sucking often gradually drift back. When they do, the reemergence of the old habit can be frustrating. Children can begin to feel that eliminating sucking forever is a hopeless goal. Parents can help with supportive reassurance. They can explain that winning the war of the thumb may take a series of battles, but that each successive battle will be easier to fight and win. They can help by re-reading the *David Decides* story, and by asking what kind of strategy their child wants to use this round.

### In addition to parents, who else can help motivate a child to quit a detrimental sucking pattern?

Occasionally parents begin to feel that nothing they or their child are doing is working. If the habit is one that is clearly damaging, and particularly if attempts at ending the habit are continuing to yield parent-child battles, bringing in a third party such as a dentist, a physician, a psychologist, or a teacher can make a big difference.

Dentists can show a child pictures or molds of teeth that have been pushed by thumbsucking. They also can offer the use of intraoral (within the mouth) appliances that block sucking. For children who want to end the habit but have not been successful with other techniques, these appliances can be very helpful.

A pediatrician, family physician, psychologist or teacher also can neutralize the situation by explaining the long-term effects of continued thumbsucking, bypassing the element of parent-child conflict.

Occasionally, involvement of a professional may cause the child to believe a parent-professional coalition is trying to overpower him. This difficulty can usually be prevented if the professional speaks directly to the child. In bypassing the parents, the professional places responsibility for breaking the habit directly on the child, and communicates a vital message of confidence that the child can overcome the impulse to suck.

### Should I ask our child's dentist to insert an appliance to stop my child's sucking habit?

As mentioned earlier, dentists can insert dental devices in the mouth to prevent sucking. Some dental researchers have reported excellent outcomes with these devices. Other dentists find the results disappointing. They report that the devices initially feel awkward to the child, and sometimes interfere with eating and speech. Appliances can be pulled out of the mouth, damaging tooth and gum tissue. As they come loose, decay can develop in teeth. Hostility engendered by the device can spoil the quality of the relationship between child and dentist and foster antagonism toward parents. Sucking may still continue. On the other hand, in many cases these difficulties do not develop and sucking is eliminated.

The critical element seems to be the child's attitude. When children want to end the sucking, these devices can help them, especially if the dentist's style engages the child's confidence and cooperation.

### Why make an issue of sucking rather than wait for children to outgrow it spontaneously?

Many children do progressively lose interest in sucking and their habit gradually disappears. Others stop suddenly on their own, perhaps because some event has convinced them that they are too old for such a "babyish" habit. Unfortunately, by the time children stop on their own, damage may already have occurred. Unnecessarily prolonged years of sucking can deform the mouth, jaws, teeth, and lips and can be detrimental to the child's sense of self-respect and social acceptability. If parents take an active role in limiting sucking when the child is young, and bring it to a halt before children enter first grade, such problems can be avoided.

## What factors indicate that a sucking habit needs to be stopped?

In general, a child's age, plus the frequency, intensity, and duration of sucking determine whether sucking habits are likely to become detrimental. The older the child, and the more time spent sucking, the more parents need to take heed.

A dentist can clarify the extent to which a child's sucking is likely to be affecting his mouth formation. By looking at a child's teeth, dentists can usually predict whether there is a vulnerability to changes from sucking. Well-aligned teeth seem to be affected less by sucking habits. Sucking has more severe impact the more the teeth are out of line to begin with.

Teachers can help parents by assessing if a child's sucking habits are interfering with healthy social or verbal development. Starting in a new school may be a positive time for growing out of old habits.

## Can parents become overly concerned about their children's sucking habits?

Absolutely. Thoughtful evaluation of sucking patterns is helpful, but anxious, guilty, angry, or alarmist responses can create additional problems. An exaggerated sense of urgency can result in overly forceful, nagging, critical, or punitive attempts at solution. Over-involvement in the child's struggle makes parents become too emotional. They may then add to the child's frustration and inhibit progress. Good-humored patience and persistence work best.

Parents can keep sucking problems in perspective if they bear in mind that sucking habits are a relatively routine concern that do not merit panic, yet a serious enough concern to merit active attention.

# Summing Up:
# Guidelines for Responding
# to Thumbsucking Children

**Infants**
Sucking is common, harmless, and beneficial for self-soothing. Enjoy watching your baby grow.

**Toddlers**
Sucking habits add to the ability to self-soothe, and tend to enhance self-reliance and self-confidence. Still, to prevent later problems, excessive daytime sucking can be minimized.
1. Offer alternatives that respond to the underlying causes.
   - Food when children are hungry
   - Naps or bedtime for tired children
   - Activity for boredom
   - Hugs and then talking about distresses
2. Limit availability of props that trigger sucking with the rule "Blankets and soft toys stay in the bedroom."

**Preschoolers**
The gains from sucking are beginning to wane, and the costs are beginning to emerge. The following warning signs indicate a sucking habit that may need to be halted.
   - Look closely when your child is sucking. Do the teeth protrude or twist, or the lips seem flared, molded around the digit?
   - Is your child developing a callous or infection on the sucking thumb or finger?

- If a finger is sucked, is it growing normally or does it appear twisted or in some other way different from the same finger on the other hand?
- Is the sucking continued vigorously throughout the night?

**School-age children**

Sucking no longer brings significant benefits. It's time to help your child end the habit.

## Footnotes

1. Goldson, Ed. "Non-Nutritive Sucking in the Sick Infant." Unpublished manuscript, available from Dr. Goldson at the Children's Hospital, Denver, CO.

2. Anderson, G. C. "Pacifiers: The Positive Side." Maternal and Child Nursing, March/April 1986, 122–124.

3. Levine, M. I., and Bell, A. I. "The Treatment of Colic in Infancy By Use of the Pacifier." Journal of Pediatrics, 37: 750–755, November 1950.

4. Paret, I. "Night Waking and its Relation to Mother-infant Interaction in Nine-month-old Infants." Frontiers of Infant Psychiatry, 1983, 171–177.

5. Paret, I. Ibid.

6. Mahalski, P. A. "The Incidence of Attachment Objects and Oral Habits at Bedtime in Two Longitudinal Samples of Children Aged 1.5 to 7 Years." Journal of Child Psychology and Psychiatry, Volume 24, Number 2, 1983. Pergamon Press Ltd., 283–295.

7. Friman, P. C. "Concurrent Habits: What Would Linus Do with His Blanket if His Thumbsucking Were Treated?" American Journal of Diseases of Children, Volume 144, December 1990, 1316–1318.

8. Massler, M. "Oral Habits: Development and Management." Journal of Pedodontics, Volume 7, Winter 1983.

9. Campbell Reid, D. A., and Price, A. H. K. "Digital Deformities and Dental Malocclusion Due to Finger Sucking." British Journal of Plastic Surgery, 37, 1984, 445–452.

10. Rankin, E. A., Jabaley, M. E., Blair, S. J., and Fraser, K. D. "Acquired Rotational Digital Deformity in Children As a Result of Finger Sucking." Journal of Hand Surgery, Volume 13A, Number 4, July 1988.

11. Bloem, J. J. A., Kon, M., and de Graaf, F. H. "Rotational Deformity of the Index Finger Caused by Reversed Finger Sucking." Annals of Plastic Surgery, Volume 21, 1988.

12. Campbell Reid, D. A., and Price, A. H. K. Op. cit.

13. Davidson, P. O., Haryett, R. D., Sandilands, M., and Hansen, F. C. "Thumbsucking: Habit or Symptom?" Journal of Dentistry for Children, Volume 34, 1967, 252–259.

14. Hughes-Davies, T. H. Letter to the editor, The Lancet, Volume 2, December 1, 1973, 1268–1269.

15. Lin-Fu, J. S. "Vulnerability of Children to Lead Exposure and Toxicity." New England Journal of Medicine, Volume 289, Number 24, 1973.

16. Tryon, A. F. "Thumb-sucking and Manifest Anxiety: A Note." Child Development, Volume 39, 1968.

17. Leung, A. K. C., and Robson, W. L. M. "Thumb Sucking." Journal of Family Practice, Volume 44, Number 5, November 1991, 1724–1728.

18. Friman, P. C., and Schmitt, M. D. "Thumb Sucking: Pediatricians' Guidelines." Clinical Pediatrics, Volume 28, Number 10, 1989, 438–440.

19. DeLaCruz, M., and Geboy, M. J. "Elimination of Thumbsucking Through Contingency Management." Journal of Dentistry for Children, January-February 1983, 39–41.

20. Gellin, M. E. "Digital Sucking and Tongue Thrusting in Children." Dental Clinics North America, Volume 22, 1978, 603–619.

21. Friman, P. C., and Schmitt, M. D. Op. cit.

22. Curzon, M. E. J. "Dental Implications of Thumbsucking." Pediatrics, Volume 54, Number 2, August 1974.

23. Popovitch, F. "The Incidence of Sucking Habits and its Relationship to Occlusion in 3-year-old Children in Burlington." Progress Report Series #1, Division of Dental Research, University of Toronto, 1956.

24. Schneider, P. E., and Peterson, J. "Oral Habits: Considerations in Management." Pediatric Clinics of North America, Volume 29, Number 3, June 1982.

25. Sheldon, G. H. "Psychological Factors in the Etiology of Malocclusion." New York State Dental Journal, Volume 35, May 1969.

26. Fletcher, B. T. "Etiology of Fingersucking: Review of Literature." Journal of Dentistry for Children, Volume 42, July–August 1975, 293–298.

27. Haryett, R. D., Hansen, F. C., and Davidson, P. O. "Chronic Thumbsucking: A Second Report on Treatment and Its Psychological Effects." American Journal of Orthodontics, Volume 57, 1970, 164–178.

28. Davidson, P. O., Haryett, R. D., Sandilands, M., and Hansen, F. C. Op. cit.

29. Levitas, T. C. "Examine the Habit—Evaluate the Treatment." Journal of Dentistry for Children. Volume 37, March–April 1970.

30. Azrin, N. H., Nunn. R. G., and Frantz-Renshaw, S. "Habit Reversal Treatment of Thumbsucking." Behauiour Research & Therapy, Volume 18, Pergamon Press Ltd, 1980, 395–399.

## Additional References

Brenchlev, M.L. "Is Digit Sucking of Significance?" *British Dentistry Journal,* Volume 171, Number 11-12, December 1991, 357-362.

Castiglia, P.T. "Thumb Sucking." *Journal of Pediatric Health Care,* Volume 2, Number 6, Nov-Dec 1988, 322-323.

Christensen, A.p., and Sanders, M.R. "Habit Reversal and Differential Reinforcement of Other Behavior in the Treatment of Thumb-sucking: An analysis of Generalization and side-effects." *Journal of Child Psychology and Psychiatry,* Volume 28, Number 2, March 1987, 281-295.

da Silva Filho, O.G., and Gomes Gloncalves, R.J. "Sucking Habits: Clinical Management in Dentistry." *Journal of Clinical Pediatrics,* Volume 15, Number 3, Spring 1991, 137-56.

Friman, P.C., and Leibowitc, J.M. "An effective and acceptable treatment alternative for chronic thmb- and finger-sucking." *Journal of Pediatric Psychology,* Volume 15, Number 1, February 1990, 57-65.

Friman, P.C., and Hove, G. "Apparent Covariation Between Child Habit Disorders: Effects of Successful Treatment for Thumb sucking on Untargeted Chronic Hair Pulling." *Journal of Applied Behavior Analysis,* Volume 20, Number 4, Winter 1987, 421-425.

Friman, P.C., Larzelere, R.E. and Finney, J.W. "Exploring the Relationship Between Thumb-sucking and Psychopathology." *Journal of Pediatric Psychology,* Volume 19, Number 4, August 1994, 431-441.

Geis, A.H., and Piarulle, D.H. "Psychological Aspects of Prolonged Thumbsucking Habits." *Journal of Clinical Orthodontics,* Volume 22, Number 8, August 1988, 492-495.

Larsson, E. "The effect of Finger-Sucking on the O cclusion: A Review." *European Journal of Orthodontics,* Volume 9, Number 4, November 1987, 270-282.

Larsson, E. "The Prevalence and Aetiology of Prolonged Dummy and Finger-Sucking Habits." *European Journal of Orthodontics,* Volume 7, Number 3, August 1985, 172-176.

Lauterbach, W. "Situation-response (S-R) questions for identifying the function of problem behavior: the example of thumb sucking." *British Journal of Psychology,* Volume 29, Part 1, February 1990, 51-57.

Lindner, A. "Relation Between Sucking Habits and Deental Characteristics in Preschool Children with Unilateral Cross-Bites." *Scandinavian Journal of Dental Research,* Volume 97, Number 3, 278-283.

Luciano, M.C., Vilchez, F. and Herruzo, J. "Say-do and Thumbsucking Behavior." *Child and Family Behavior Therapy*, Volume 14, Number 1, 1992, 63-69.

Macauley, M. "Hypnosis and Story-Telling. A remedy for thumg sucking." Ont Dentistry, Volume 97, Number 9, November 1990, 43-44.

Rinchuse, D.J. "Overcoming Fingersucking Habits." *Journal of Clincal Orthodontics*, Volume 20, Number 1, January 1986, 46-47.

Singhal, P.K., Bhatia, M.S., Nigam, V.r., and Bohra, N. "Thumb Sucking: An Analysis of 150 Cases." *Indian Pediatrics*, Volume 25, Number 7, July 1988, 647-653.

Van, Houten R. and Rolider, A. "The Use of Response Prevention to Eliminate Nocturnal Thumbsucking." *Journal of Applied Behavior Analysis*, Volume 17, Number 4, Winter 1984, 509-520.

VanNorman, R.A. "Digit Sucking: It's Time for an Attitude Adjustment or a Rationale For the Early Elimination of Digit-Sucking Habits Through Positive Bahavior Modifications." *International Journal of Orofacial Myology*, Volume 11, Number 2, July 1985, 14-21.

Wolf, A.W., and Lozoff, B. "Object Attachment, Thumbsucking, and the Passage to Sleep." *Journal of the American Academy of Child Adolescent Psychiatry*, Volume 28, Number 2, 287-292.

Yoshida, Y., Ohno, T., and Shikano, R. "An Approach to digitsucking cases. Part One. Consideration of methods of instruction for digitsucking cases." *International Journal of Orofacial Myology*, Volume 17, Number 1, March 1991, 5-9.